THIS COLORING BOOK BELONGS TO

_____

FISH

FISH

ALLIGATOR

ALLIGATOR

BEE

BEE

ELEPHANT

CHICK

CHICK

LION

LION

CAT

CAT

GIRAFFE

BEAR

BEAR

DUCK

DUCK

HIPPOPOTAMUS

HIPPOPOTAMUS

GUINEA PIG

GUINEA PIG

KOALA BEAR

LIZARD

LIZARD

DOLPHIN

DOLPHIN

GOAT

GOAT

PARROT

PARROT

RABBIT

RABBIT

DOG

DOG

EAGLE

EAGLE

ZEBRA

ZEBRA

PORCUPINE

PORCUPINE

KANGAROO

KANGAROO

SNAKE

TIGER

TIGER

MONKEY

MONKEY

RACCOON

RACCOON

BULL

BULL

SHARK

SHARK

PENGUIN

OWL

OWL

CAMEL

CAMEL

GORILLA

GORILLA

SEAHORSE

SEAHORSE

RHINOCEROS

RHINOCEROS

FOX

FOX

PIG

TURTLE

TURTLE

SHEEP

SHEEP

WHALE

PANDA

PANDA

SEAL

SEAL

DEER

DEER

CRAB

CRAB

PONY

PONY

BIRD

RAM

RAM

TURKEY

TURKEY

FLAMINGO

FLAMINGO

COW

COW

LLAMA

LLAMA

SQUIRREL

SQUIRREL